BUG AWFUL

BUG AWFUL

EDITED BY

Isaac Asimov

Martin Harry Greenberg

Charles Waugh

ILLUSTRATED

William Ersland

♣ RAINTREE PUBLISHERS

MILWAUKEE TORONTO MELBOURNE LONDON

ℬ BLACKWELL RAINTREE

OXFORD

Library of Congress Number: 83-21309

1 2 3 4 5 6 7 8 9 87 86 85 84

Printed and bound in the United States of America.

Library of Congress Cataloging in Publication Data

Main entry under title:

Bug awful.
   (Science fiction shorts)
   Contents: Introduction / Isaac Asimov—Mimic / Donald A.
Wollheim—The useless bugbreeders / James Stamers—[etc.]
   1. Science fiction.   2. Children's stories.
[1. Science fiction.   2. Short stories]   I. Asimov, Isaac, 1920-
II. Greenberg, Martin Harry. III. Waugh, Charles.   IV. Ersland, Bill, ill.
V. Series.
PZ5.B86 1984   [Fic]   83-21309

U.S. ISBN   0-8172-1739-8   (lib. bdg.)
U.K. SBN 0-86256-126-4

Published simultaneously in the U.K. by Blackwell Raintree.

Contents

Introduction

ISAAC ASIMOV

I suppose that if any of you were asked which is the most successful form of life that ever lived, you might say "human beings."

Human beings, with their tools and weapons, are more powerful than any other kind (or "species") of animal. There are many animals that can kill unarmed human beings, and some might be dangerous even to a single armed human being. However, get a number of human beings together with the proper weapons, and they can wipe out any number of large and dangerous animals.

In fact, it is possible that in a few decades, all the large animals *will* be wiped out except for those that are kept on nature preserves and in zoos. This might be so even though governments are trying to preserve such animals as African elephants, rhinoceroses, whooping cranes, California condors, and so on.

In fact, if human beings ever decide to have a nuclear war, they may even wipe out themselves.

And yet there are animals against which we seem to be helpless and which are, in some ways, much more successful than we are. Consider the insects—the little bugs all about us.

Do you know that there are about a million different species of insects that are known and named? Do you know that if you were to list all the various species of animals there are, from the largest whales to the tiniest one-celled amebas, five out of every six species would be insects? Do you know that scientists expect there are anywhere from one million to four million animal species that have not yet been discovered and studied and that almost all of them are probably insects?

Why is that? Insects are very small and very fecund; that is, they give birth to many, many young. All these young vary slightly among themselves and only a small fraction grow to maturity. Those that do grow to maturity tend to be those with variations that help them fit their environments. That means that insects evolve very quickly and split up into different varieties and sub-varieties until there are hundreds of thousands of different species, each of which lives in a different way, on different food. They fill the earth.

Naturally, most of them die. They are eaten by the millions by birds and by small animals of all kinds, but there are always a few left, and these breed so quickly that if other animals just look the other way for a little while, the numbers are restored.

Even human beings are helpless. They don't eat insects, but they do try to kill them, and it's not just a matter of a flyswatter. Human beings have discovered chemicals that kill insects, for instance. For a while, these insecticides slaughter vast numbers, but there are always some insects that survive, often because they just happen to be naturally resistant to the insecticides. These few survivors then have enormous numbers of offspring, all, or most, of which are similarly resistant. The numbers are restored, and human beings have to find a new way of doing them in.

Although human beings are wiping out many species of mammals, birds, and other kinds of creatures, it is said that human beings have never been successful in wiping out a single species of insect.

Most insects are quite useful in one way or another. Bees give us honey, the silkworm gives us silk, and so on. Even insects that aren't directly useful to us are important because they serve as a food supply for birds, or because they fertilize plants, or because they scavenge dead organisms.

Just the same, there are a few that are dangerous, that spread disease, that bite and harass us, that eat vast quantities of our crops. We've been fighting them uselessly all through history and perhaps when we've had our nuclear war and destroyed civilization, it will be the insects who will continue onward exactly as before, inheriting the Earth we have so foolishly given up.

So bugs make interesting characters in science fiction stories—usually as villians.

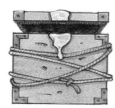

Mimic

DONALD A. WOLLHEIM

It is less than five hundred years since an entire half of the world was discovered. It is less than two hundred years since the discovery of the last continent. The sciences of chemistry and physics go back scarcely one century. The science of aviation goes back about seventy-five years. The science of space is being born.

And yet we think we know a lot.

We know little or nothing. Some of the most startling things are unknown to us. When they are discovered, they may shock us to the bone.

We search for secrets in the far islands of the Pacific and among the ice fields of the frozen North, while under our very noses, rubbing shoulders with us every day, there may walk the undiscovered. It is a curious fact of nature that that which is in plain view is often best hidden.

I have always known of the man in the black cloak. Since I was a child he has always lived on my street, and his eccentricities are so familiar that they go unmentioned except among the casual visitor. Here, in the heart of one of the largest cities in the world, in swarming New York, the eccentric and the odd may flourish unhindered.

As children we had hilarious fun jeering at the man in black when he displayed his fear of women. We watched, in our evil, childish way, for those moments, we tried to get him to show anger. But he ignored us completely and soon we paid him no further heed, even as our parents did.

We saw him only twice a day. Once in the early morning—when we would see his six-foot figure come out of the grimy dark hallway of the tenement at the end of the street and stride down toward the elevated to work—and again when he came back at night. He was always dressed in a long, black cloak that came to his ankles, and he wore a wide-brimmed black hat down far over his face. He was a sight from some weird story out of the old lands. But he harmed nobody, and paid attention to nobody.

Nobody—except perhaps women.

When a woman crossed his path, he would stop in his stride and come to a dead halt. We could see that he closed his eyes until she had passed. Then he would snap those wide, watery blue eyes open and march on as if nothing had happened.

He was never known to speak to a woman. He would buy some groceries, maybe once a week, at Antonio's—but only when there were no other patrons there. Antonio said once that he never talked, he just pointed at things he wanted and paid for them in bills that he pulled out of a pocket somewhere under his cloak. Antonio did not like him, but he never had any trouble from him either.

He never had visitors, he never spoke to anyone. And he had once built something in his room out of metal.

He had once, years ago, hauled up some long flat metal sheets, sheets of tin or iron, and they had heard a lot of hammering and banging in his room for several days. But that had stopped and that was all there was to that story.

Where he worked I don't know and never found out. He had money, for he was reputed to pay his rent regularly when the janitor asked for it.

Well, people like that inhabit big cities and nobody knows the stories of their lives until they're all over. Or until something strange happens.

I grew up, I went to college, I studied.

Finally I got a job assisting a museum curator. I spent my days mounting beetles and classifying exhibits of stuffed animals and preserved plants, and hundreds and hundreds of insects from all over.

Nature is a strange thing, I learned. You learn that very clearly when you work in a museum. You realize how nature uses the art of camouflage. There are twig insects that look exactly like a leaf or a branch of a tree. Exactly.

Nature is strange and perfect that way. There is a moth in Central America that looks like a wasp. It even has a fake stinger made of hair, which it twists and curls just like a wasp's stinger. It has the same colorings and, even though its body is soft and not armored like a wasp's, it is colored to appear shiny and armored. It even flies in the daytime when wasps do, and not at night like all other moths. It moves like a wasp. It knows somehow that it is helpless and that it can survive only by pretending to be as deadly to other insects as wasps are.

I learned about army ants, and their strange imitators.

Army ants travel in huge columns of thousands and hundreds of thousands. They move along in a flowing stream several yards across and they eat everything in their path. Everything in the jungle is afraid of them. Wasps, bees, snakes, other ants, birds, lizards, beetles—even men run away, or get eaten.

But in the midst of the army ants there also travel many other creatures—creatures that aren't ants at all, and that the army ants would kill if they knew of them. But they don't know of them because these other creatures are disguised. Some of them are beetles that look like ants. They have false markings like ant thoraxes and they run along in imitation of ant speed. There is even one that is so long it is marked like three ants in single file! It moves so fast that the real ants never give it a second glance.

There are weak caterpillars that look like big armored beetles. There are all sorts of things that look like dangerous animals. Animals that are the killers and superior fighters of their groups have no enemies. The army ants and the wasps, the sharks, the hawk, and the felines. So there are a host of weak things that try to hide among them—to mimic them.

And people are the greatest killers, the greatest hunters of them all. The whole world of nature knows humans as the irresistible masters. The roar of a gun, the cunning of a trap, the strength and agility of an arm place all else beneath them.

Should humans then be treated by nature differently from the other dominants, the army ants and the wasps?

It was, as often happens to be the case, sheer luck that I happened to be on the street at the dawning hour when the janitor came running out of the tenement on my street shouting for help. I had been working all night mounting new exhibits.

The policeman on the beat and I were the only people besides the janitor to see the thing that we found in the two dingy rooms occupied by the stranger of the black cloak.

The janitor explained—as the officer and I dashed up the narrow, rickety stairs—that he had been awakened by the sound of heavy thuds and shrill screams in the stranger's rooms. He had gone out in the hallway to listen.

When we got there, the place was silent. A faint light shone from under the doorway. The policeman knocked, there was no answer. He put his ear to the door and so did I. We heard a faint rustling—a continuous slow rustling as of a breeze blowing paper.

The policeman knocked again, but there was still no response.

Then, together, we threw our weight at the door. Two hard blows and the rotten old lock gave way. We burst in.

The room was filthy, the floor covered with scraps of torn paper, bits of detritus and garbage. The room was unfurnished, which I thought was odd.

In the corner there stood a metal box, about four feet square. A tight box, held together with screws and ropes. It had a lid, opening at the top, which was down and fastened with a sort of wax seal.

The stranger of the black cloak lay in the middle of the floor—dead.

He was still wearing the cloak. The big slouch hat was lying on the floor some distance away. From the inside of the box the faint rustling was coming.

We turned the stranger over and took the cloak off. For several instants we saw nothing amiss and then gradually— horribly—we became aware of some things that were wrong.

His hair was short and curly brown. It stood straight up in its inch-long length. His eyes were open and staring. I noticed first that he had no eyebrows, only a curious dark line in the flesh over each eye.

It was then I realized he had no nose. But no one had ever noticed that before. His skin was oddly mottled. Where the nose should have been there were dark shadowings that made the appearance of a nose, if you only just glanced at him. Like the work of a skillful artist in a painting.

His mouth was as it should be and slightly open—but he had no teeth. His head perched upon a thin neck.

The suit was . . . not a suit. It was part of him. It was his body.

What we thought was a coat was a huge black wing sheath, like a beetle has. He had a thorax like an insect, only the wing sheath covered it and you couldn't notice it when he wore the cloak. The body bulged out below, tapering off into the two long, thin hind legs. His arms came out from under the top of the "coat." He had a tiny secondary pair of arms folded tightly across his chest. There was a sharp, round hole newly pierced in his chest just above the arms, still oozing a watery liquid.

The janitor fled gibbering. The officer was pale but standing by his duty.

The sight was a shock such that leaves one in full control. The mind rejects it, and it is only in afterthought that one can feel the dim shudder of horror.

The rustling was still coming from the box. I motioned to the white-faced officer and we went over and stood before it. He took the nightstick and knocked away the waxen seal.

Then we heaved and pulled the lid open.

A wave of noxious vapor assailed us. We staggered back as suddenly a stream of flying things shot out of the huge iron container. The window was open, and straight out into the first glow of dawn they flew.

There must have been dozens of them. They were about two or three inches long and they flew on wide gauzy beetle wings. They looked like little men, strangely terrifying as they flew— clad in their black suits, with their expressionless faces and their dots of watery blue eyes. And they flew out on transparent wings that came from under their black beetle coats.

I ran to the window, fascinated, almost hypnotized. The horror of it had not reached my mind at once. Afterward I have had spasms of numbing terror as my mind tries to put the things together. The whole business was so utterly unexpected.

We know of army ants and their imitators, yet it never occurred to us that we too were army ants of a sort. We knew of stick insects and it never occurred to us that there might be others that disguise themselves to fool, not other animals, but the supreme animals themselves—humans.

We found some bones in the bottom of that iron case afterwards. But we couldn't identify them. Perhaps we did not try very hard. They might have been human. . . .

I suppose the stranger of the black cloak did not fear women so much as it distrusted them. Women notice men, perhaps, more closely than other men do. Women might become suspicious sooner of the inhumanity, the deception. And then there might perhaps have been some touch of instinctive feminine jealousy. The stranger was disguised as a man, but its sex was surely female. The things in the box were its young.

But it is the other thing I saw when I ran to the window that has shaken me the most. The policeman did not see it. Nobody else saw it but me, and I only for an instant.

When I went to the window, I saw the small cloud of flying things rising up into the sky and sailing away into the purple distance. The dawn was breaking and the first rays of the sun were just striking over the housetops.

Shaken, I looked away from the fourth-floor tenement room over the roofs of lower buildings. Chimneys and walls and empty clotheslines made the scenery over which the tiny mass of horror passed.

And then I saw a chimney, not thirty feet away on the next roof. It was squat and of red brick and had two black pipe ends flush with its top. I saw it suddenly vibrate, oddly. And I saw its red brick surface seem to peel away, and the black pipe openings suddenly turn white.

A great, flat-winged thing detached itself silently from the surface of the real chimney and darted after the cloud of flying things.

I watched until all had lost themselves in the sky.

Meddler

PHILIP K. DICK

They entered the great chamber. At the far end, technicians hovered around an immense illuminated board, following a complex pattern of lights that shifted rapidly, flashing through seemingly endless combinations. At long tables machines whirred—computers, human-operated and robot. Wall-charts covered every inch of vertical space. Hasten gazed around him in amazement.

Wood laughed. "Come over here and I'll really show you something. You recognize *this*, don't you?" He pointed to a hulking machine surrounded by silent men and women in white lab robes.

"I recognize it," Hasten said slowly. "It's something like our own Dip, but perhaps twenty times larger. What do you haul up? And *when* do you haul?" He fingered the surface-plate of the Dip, then squatted down, peering into the maw. The maw was locked shut; the Dip was in operation. "You know, if we had any idea this existed, Histo-Research would have—"

"You know now." Wood bent down beside him. "Listen, Hasten, you're the first man from outside the Department ever to get into this room. You saw the guards. No one gets in unauthorized; here the guards have orders to kill anyone trying to enter illegally."

"To hide this? A machine? You'd shoot to—"

They stood, Wood facing him, his jaw hard. "*Your* Dip digs back into antiquity. Rome. Greece. Dust and old volumes." Wood touched the big Dip beside them. "This Dip is different.

17

We guard it with our lives, and anyone else's lives. Do you know why?"

Hasten stared at it.

"This Dip is set, not for antiquity, but—for the future." Wood looked directly into Hasten's face. "Do you understand? The future?"

"You're dredging the future? But you can't! It's forbidden by law; you know that!" Hasten drew back. "If the Executive Council knew this they'd break this building apart. You know the dangers. Berkowsky himself demonstrated them in his original thesis."

Hasten paced angrily. "I can't understand you, using a future-oriented Dip. When you pull material from the future you automatically introduce new factors into the present; the future is altered—you start a never-ending shift. The more you dip the more new factors are brought in. You create unstable conditions for centuries to come. That's why the law was passed."

Wood nodded. "I know."

"And you still keep dipping?" Hasten gestured at the machine and the technicians. "Stop, for God's sake! Stop before you introduce some lethal element that can't be erased. Why do you keep—"

Wood sagged suddenly. "All right, Hasten, don't lecture us. It's too late; it's already happened. A lethal factor was introduced into our first experiments. We thought we knew what we were doing. . . ." He looked up. "And that's why you were brought here. Sit down—you're going to hear all about it."

"Please start at the beginning," Hasten said.

"The Dip was authorized by the Political Science Council. They wanted to know the results of some of their decisions. At first we objected, giving Berkowsky's theory; but the idea is hypnotic, you know. We gave in, and the Dip was built—secretly, of course.

"We made our first dredge about one year hence. To protect ourselves against Berkowsky's factor we tried a subterfuge; we actually brought nothing back. This Dip is geared to pick up nothing. No object is scooped; it merely photographs from a high altitude. The film comes back to us and we make enlargements and try to gestalt the conditions.

"Results were all right, at first. No more wars, cities growing, much better looking. Blow-ups of street scenes show many people, well-content, apparently. Pace a little slower.

"Then we went ahead fifty years. Even better: cities on the decrease. People not so dependent on machines. More grass, parks. Same general conditions, peace, happiness, much leisure. Less frenetic waste, hurry.

"We went on, skipping ahead. Of course, with such an indirect viewing method we couldn't be certain of anything, but it all looked fine. We relayed out information to the Council and they went ahead with their planning. And then it happened."

"What, exactly?" Hasten said, leaning forward.

"We decided to revisit a period we had already photographed, about a hundred years hence. We sent out the Dip, got it back with a full reel. The men developed it and we watched the run." Wood paused.

"And?"

"And it wasn't the same. It was different. Everything was changed. War—war and destruction everywhere." Wood shuddered. "We were appalled. We sent the Dip back at once to make absolutely certain."

"And what did you find this time?"

Wood's fists clenched. "Changed again, and for the worse! Ruins, vast ruins. People poking around. Ruin and death everywhere. Slag. The *end* of the war, the last phase."

"I see," Hasten said, nodding.

"That's not the worst! We conveyed the news to the Council. It ceased all activity and went into a two-week conference. It canceled all ordinances and withdrew every plan formed on the basis of our reports. It was a month before the Council got in touch with us again. The members wanted us to try once more, take one more Dip to the same period. We said no, but they insisted. It could be no worse, they argued.

"So we sent the Dip out again. It came back and we ran the film. Hasten, there are things worse than war. You wouldn't believe what we saw. There was no human life; none at all, not a single human being."

"Everything was destroyed?"

"No! No destruction, cities big and stately, roads, buildings, lakes, fields. But no human life. The cities empty, functioning mechanically, every machine and wire untouched. But no living people."

"What was it?"

"We sent the Dip on ahead, at fifty year leaps. Nothing. Nothing each time. Cities, roads, buildings, but no human life. Everyone dead. Plague, radiation, or what, we don't know. But *something* killed them. Where did it come from? We don't know. It wasn't there at first, not in our original dips.

"Somehow, *we* introduced it, the lethal factor. *We* brought it, with our meddling. It wasn't there when we started it. It was done by us, Hasten." Wood stared at him, his face a white mask. "We brought it and now we've got to find what it is and get rid of it."

"How are you going to do that?"

"We've built a Time Car, capable of carrying one human observer into the future. We're sending a man there to see what it is. Photographs don't tell us enough; we have to know more! When did it first appear? How? What were the first signs? *What is it?* Once we know, maybe we can eliminate it, the factor, trace it down and remove it. Someone must go into the future and find out what it was we began. It's the only way."

Wood stood up, and Hasten rose, too.

"You're that person," Wood said. "You're going, the most competent person available. The Time Car is outside, in an open square, carefully guarded." Wood gave a signal. Two soldiers came toward the desk.

"Come with us," Wood said. "We're going outside to the square; make sure no one follows after us." He turned to Hasten. "Ready?"

Hasten hesitated. "Wait a minute. I'll have to go over your work, study what's been done. Examine the Time Car itself. I can't—"

The two soldiers moved closer, looking to Wood. Wood put his hand on Hasten's shoulder. "I'm sorry," he said, "we have no time to waste. Come along with me."

All around him blackness moved, swirling toward him and then receding. He sat down on the stool before the bank of controls, wiping the perspiration from his face. He was on his way, for better or worse. Briefly, Wood had outlined the operation of the Time Car. A few moments of instruction, the controls set for him, and then the metal door slammed behind him.

Hasten looked around him. It was cold in the sphere; the air was thin and chilly. He watched the moving dials for a while, but presently the cold began to make him uncomfortable. He went over to the equipment-locker and slid the door back. A jacket, a heavy jacket, and a flash gun. He held the gun for a minute, studying it. And tools, all kinds of tools and equipment. He was just putting the gun away when the dull chugging under him suddenly ceased. For one terrible second he was floating, drifting aimlessly, then the feeling was gone.

Sunlight flowed through the window, spreading out over the floor. He snapped the artificial lights off and went to the window to see. Wood had set the controls for a hundred years hence: bracing himself, he looked out.

A meadow, flowers and grass, rolling off into the distance. Blue sky and wandering clouds. Some animals grazed a long way off, standing together in the shade of a tree. He went to the door and unlocked it, stepping out. Warm sunlight struck him, and he felt better at once. Now he could see the animals were cows.

He went back and got the gun from the locker. Then he returned to the lip of the sphere, checked the door-lock to be certain it would remain closed during his absence. Only then, Hasten stepped down onto the grass of the meadow. He closed the door and looked around him. Presently he began to walk quickly away from the sphere, toward the top of a long hill that stretched out half a mile away. As he strode along, he examined the click-band on his wrist which would guide him back to the metal sphere, the Time Car, if he could not find the way himself.

He came to the cows, passing by their tree. The cows got up and moved away from him. He noticed something that gave him a sudden chill. Their udders were small and wrinkled.

Not herd cows.

When he reached the top of the hill he stopped, lifting his glasses from his waist. The earth fell away, mile after mile of it, dry green fields without pattern or design, rolling like waves as far as the eye could see. Nothing else? He turned, sweeping the horizon.

He stiffened, adjusting the sight. Far off to the left, at the very limit of vision, the vague perpendiculars of a city rose up. He lowered the glasses and hitched up his heavy boots. Then he walked down the other side of the hill, taking big steps. He had a long way to go.

Hasten had not walked more than half an hour when he saw butterflies. They rose up suddenly a few yards in front of him, dancing and fluttering in the sunlight. He stopped to rest, watching them. They were all colors, red and blue, with splashes of yellow and green. They were the largest butterflies he had ever seen. Perhaps they had come from some zoo, escaped and bred wild after man left the scene. The butterflies rose higher and higher in the air. They took no notice of him but struck out toward the distant spires of the city. In a moment they were gone.

Hasten started up again. It was hard to imagine the death of man in such circumstances, butterflies and grass and cows in the shade. What a quiet and lovely world was left, without the human race!

Suddenly one last butterfly fluttered up, almost to his face, rising quickly from the grass. He put his arm up automatically, batting at it. The butterfly dashed against his hand. He began to laugh—

Pain made him sick. He fell half to his knees, gasping and retching. He rolled over on his face, hunching himself up, burying his face in the ground. His arm ached, and pain knotted him up; his head swam and he closed his eyes.

When Hasten turned over at last, the butterfly was gone. It had not lingered.

He lay for a time in the grass, then he sat up slowly, getting shakily to his feet. He stripped off his shirt and examined his hand and wrist. The flesh was black, hard and already swelling. He glanced down at it and then at the distant city. The butterflies had gone there. . . .

He made his way back to the Time Car.

Hasten reached the sphere a little after the sun had begun to drop into evening darkness. The door slid back to his touch and he stepped inside. He dressed his hand and arm with salve from the medicine kit and then sat down on the stool, deep in thought, staring at his arm. A small sting, accidental, in fact. The butterfly had not even noticed. Suppose the whole pack—

He waited until the sun had completely set and it was pitch black outside the sphere. At night all the bees and butterflies disappeared. Or at least those he knew did. Well, he would have to take a chance. His arm still ached dully, throbbing without respite. The salve had done no good. He felt dizzy, and there was a fever taste in his mouth.

Before he went out he opened the locker and brought all the things out. He examined the flash gun but put it aside. A moment later he found what he wanted. A blowtorch and a flashlight. He put all the other things back and stood up. Now he was ready—if that was the word for it. As ready as he would ever be.

He stepped out into the darkness, flashing the light ahead of him. He walked quickly. It was a dark and lonely night. Only a few stars shone above him, and his was the only earthly light. He passed up the hill and down the other side. A grove of trees loomed up, and then he was on a level plain, feeling his way toward the city by the beam of the flashlight.

When he reached the city he was very tired. He had gone a long way, and his breath was beginning to come hard. Huge ghostly outlines rose up ahead of him, disappearing above, vanishing into darkness. It was not a large city, apparently, but its design was strange to Hasten, more vertical and slim than he was used to.

He went through the gate. Grass was growing from the stone pavement of the streets. He stopped, looking down. Grass and weeds everywhere; and in the corners, by the buildings were bones, little heaps of bones and dust. He walked on, flashing his light against the sides of the slender buildings. His footsteps echoed hollowly. There was no light except his own.

The buildings began to thin out. Soon he found himself entering a great tangled square, overgrown with bushes and vines. At the far end a building larger than the others rose. He walked toward it, across the empty, desolate square, flashing his light from side to side. He walked up a half-buried step and onto a concrete plaza. All at once he stopped. To his right, another building reared up, catching his attention. His heart thudded. Above the doorway his light made out a word cut expertly into the arch: BIBLIOTHECA.

This was what he wanted, the library. He went up the steps toward the dark entrance. Wood boards gave under his feet. He reached the entrance and found himself facing a heavy wood door with metal handles. When he took hold of the handles the door fell toward him, crashing past him, down the steps and into the darkness. The odor of decay and dust choked him.

He went inside. Spider webs brushed against his helmet as he passed along silent halls. He chose a room at random and entered it. Here were more heaps of dust and gray bits of bones. Low tables and shelves ran along the walls. He went to the shelves and took down a handful of books. They powdered and broke in his hands, showering bits of paper and thread onto him. Had only a century passed since his own time?

Hasten sat down at one of the tables and opened one of the books that was in better condition. The words were no language he knew, a Romance language that he knew must be artificial. He turned page after page. At last he took a handful of books at random and moved back toward the door. Suddenly his heart jumped. He went over to the wall, his hands trembling. Newspapers.

He took the brittle, cracking sheets carefully down, holding them to the light. The same language, of course. Bold, black headlines. He managed to roll some of the papers together and add them to his load of books. Then he went through the door, out into the corridor, back the way he had come.

When he stepped out onto the steps cold fresh air struck him, tingling his nose. He looked around at the dim outlines rising up on all sides of the square. Then he walked down and across the square, feeling his way carefully along. He came to

the gate of the city, and a moment later he was outside, on the flat plain again, heading back toward the Time Car.

A cold wind moved through the air, eddying against him. In the forming gray light, the trees and hills were beginning to take shape, a hard, unbending outline. He turned toward the city. Bleak and thin, the shafts of deserted buildings stuck up. For a moment he watched, fascinated by the first color of day as it struck the shafts and towers. Then the color faded, and a drifting mist moved between him and the city. All at once he bent down and grabbed up his load. He began to walk, hurrying as best he could, chill fear moving through him.

From the city a black speck had leaped up into the sky and was hovering over it.

After a time, a long time, Hasten looked back. The speck was still there—but it had grown. And it was no longer black. In the clear light of day the speck was beginning to flash, shining with many colors.

He increased his pace; he went down the side of a hill and up another. For a second he paused to snap on his click-band. It spoke loudly; he was not far from the sphere. He waved his arm and the clicks rose and fell. To the right. Wiping the perspiration from his hands, he went on.

A few minutes later he looked down from the top of a ridge and saw a gleaming metal sphere resting silently on the grass, dripping with cold dew from the night. The Time Car. Sliding and running, he leaped down the hill toward it.

He was just pushing the door open with his shoulder when the first cloud of butterflies appeared at the top of the hill, moving quietly toward him.

He locked the door and set his armload down, flexing his muscles. His hand ached, burning now with an intense pain. He had no time for that. He hurried to the window and peered out. The butterflies were swarming toward the sphere, darting and dancing above him, flashing with color. They began to settle down onto the metal, even onto the window. Abruptly, his gaze was cut off by gleaming bodies, soft and pulpy, their beating wings mashed together. He listened. He could hear them, a muffled, echoing sound that came from all sides of him. The interior of the sphere dimmed into darkness as the

butterflies sealed off the window. He lit the artificial lights.

Time passed. He examined the newspapers, uncertain of what to do. Go back? Or go ahead? Better jump ahead fifty years or so. The butterflies were dangerous, but perhaps not the real thing, the lethal factor that he was looking for. He looked at his hand. The skin was black and hard, a dead area that was increasing. A faint shadow of worry went through him. It was getting worse, not better.

The scratching sound on all sides of him began to annoy him, filling him with an uneasy restlessness. He put down the books and paced back and forth. How could insects, even immense insects such as these, destroy the human race? Surely human beings could combat them. Dusts, poisons, sprays.

A bit of metal, a little particle drifted down onto his sleeve. He brushed it off. A second particle fell, and then some tiny fragments. He leaped, his head jerking up.

A circle was forming above his head. Another circle appeared to the right of it, and then a third. All around him circles were forming in the walls and roof of the sphere. He ran to the control board and closed the safety switch. The board hummed into life. He began to set the indicator panel, working rapidly, frantically. Now pieces of metal were dropping down, a rain of metal fragments onto the floor. Corrosive, some kind of substance exuded from them. Acid? Natural secretion of some sort. A large piece of metal fell; he turned.

Into the sphere the butterflies came, fluttering and dancing toward him. The piece that had fallen was a circle of metal, cut cleanly through. He did not have time even to notice it. He snatched up the blowtorch and snapped it on. The flame sucked and gurgled. As the butterflies came toward him he pressed the handle and held the spout up. The air burst alive with burning particles that rained down all over him, and a furious odor reeked through the sphere.

He closed the last switches. The indicator lights flickered, the floor chugged under him. He threw the main lever. More butterflies were pushing in, crowding each other eagerly, struggling to get through. A second circle of metal crashed to the floor suddenly, admitting a new horde. Hasten cringed,

backing away, the blowtorch up, spouting flame. The butter-flies came on, more and more of them.

Then sudden silence settled over everything, a quiet so abrupt that he blinked. The endless, insistent scratching had ceased. He was alone, except for a cloud of ashes and particles over the floor and walls, the remains of the butterflies that had got into the sphere. Hasten sat down on the stool, trembling. He was safe, on his way back to his own time; and there was no doubt, no possible doubt that he had found the lethal factor. It was there, in the heap of ashes on the floor, in the circles neatly cut in the hull of the Car. Corrosive secretion? He smiled grimly.

His last vision of them, of the swelling horde, had told him what he wanted to know. Clutched carefully against the first butterflies through the circles were tools, tiny cutting tools. They had cut their way in, bored through; they had come carrying their own equipment.

He sat down, waiting for the Time Car to complete its journey.

Department guards caught hold of him, helping him from the Car. He stepped down unsteadily, leaning against them. "Thanks," he murmured.

Wood hurried up. "Hasten, you're all right?"

He nodded. "Yes. Except my hand."

"Let's get inside at once." They went through the door, into the great chamber. "Sit down." Wood waved his hand impatiently, and a soldier hurried a chair over. "Get him some hot coffee."

Coffee was brought. Hasten sat sipping. At last he pushed the cup away and leaned back.

"Can you tell us now?" Wood asked.

"Yes."

"Fine." Wood sat down across from him. A tape recorder whirred into life and a camera began to photograph Hasten's face as he talked. "Go on. What did you find?"

When he had finished, the room was silent. None of the guards or technicians spoke.

Wood stood up, trembling. "God. So it's a form of toxic life that got them. I thought it was something like that. But butterflies? And intelligent. Planning attacks. Probably rapid breeding, quick adaptation."

"Maybe the books and newspapers will help us."

"But where did they come from? Mutation of some existing form? Or from some other planet. Maybe space travel brought them in. We've got to find out."

"They attacked only human beings," Hasten said. "They left the cows. Just people."

"Maybe we can stop them." Wood snapped on the vidphone. "I'll have the Council convene an emergency session. We'll give them your description and recommendations. We'll start a program, organize units all over the planet. Now that we know what it is, we have a chance. Thanks to you, Hasten, maybe we can stop them in time!"

The operator appeared and Wood gave the Council's code letter. Hasten watched dully. At last he got to his feet and wandered around the room. His arm throbbed unmercifully. Presently he went back outside, through the doorway into the open square. Some soldiers were examining the Time Car curiously. Hasten watched them without feeling, his mind blank.

"What is this, sir?" one asked.

"That?" Hasten roused himself, going slowly over. "That's a Time Car."

"No, I mean this." The soldier pointed to something on the hull. "This, sir; it wasn't on there when the Car went out."

Hasten's heart stopped beating. He pushed past them, staring up. At first he saw nothing on the metal hull, only the corroded metal surface. Then chill fright rushed through him.

Something small and brown and furry was there, on the surface. He reached out, touching it. A sack, a stiff little brown sack. It was dry, dry and empty. There was nothing in it, and it was open at one end. He stared up. All across the hull of the Car were little brown sacks, some still full, but most of them already empty.

Cocoons.

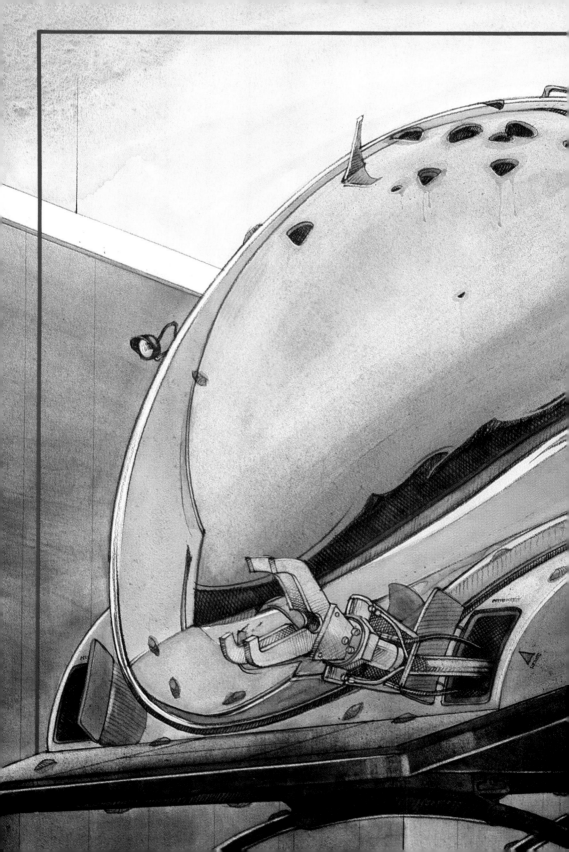

The Useless Bugbreeders

JAMES STAMERS

The previous case was a Weeper, and he lost. So the Space Zoning Commissioners were damp and irritable before I opened pleadings for my client. I tried not to squelch as I approached the bench.

"Not the Flammables again, Mr. Jones?" the fat Commissioner asked nastily, sponging his suit with a sodden handkerchief.

"That was last week, Your Honor."

The thin dark Commissioner stared pointedly at the charred end of the bench nearest the witness seat.

"Indeed it was, Mr. Jones."

The middle Commissioner poised his fingers and looked at the court ceiling; moisture gleamed diamond-like on his bald head.

"Now let me see," he intoned. "Correct me if I err, Mr. Jones, but I seem to observe you have a habit of representing somewhat spectacular aliens. Including, in the past six months alone, the Drillers, Whirling Tombs, Fragile Glasses, Erupters, Vibrational Men, Transparent Women—and of course let us not forget the Flammables."

"I assure Your Honor, my present clients will be found to be sober, hardworking, desirable members of the Galactic Community, seeking only to live on their own asteroid in peace under a democratic system, which . . ."

"Thank you, Mr. Jones. Shall we proceed?"

"And perhaps," added the fat Commissioner, "you may be good enough to leave us with most of our courtroom intact on this occasion."

The thin Commissioner sighed and shuffled his papers.

"You appear, Mr. Jones, to contest a Space Council ruling for the elimination of Asteroid Four Thousand Seven Hundred and Twenty-Two on the grounds, which you allege, that it is a peaceful dwelling of an adult and responsible alien race."

"Yes, Your Honor."

"Then let us see your adult, um, Bugbreeder."

My client hopped off the table and ran nimbly up to the witness seat. He sat there like a small green snowball with large and pointed ears.

"Happy, happy to be here, I'm sure," he said.

Fortunately he had a hand to raise and looked reasonably humanoid as he was sworn in. The caterpillar and semi-jelly cultures make a less favorable first impression, and at this point the Driller had gone excitedly through the floor.

"You are a representative member of your race?" I asked formally.

"Oh, yus. Much."

"And you reside on Asteroid Four Thousand Seven Hundred and Twenty-Two, the permanent dwelling of your race?"

"Oh, yus. Home."

"And although your home presents certain technical difficulties on the spacerun to the greater planets, you maintain it should be preserved because of your contribution to the culture of the Galactic Community?" I asked.

"Oh, yus."

"Does he understand a word you're saying, Mr. Jones?" asked the bald Commissioner.

"Oh, yus. Not much," said my client cheerfully.

"Hurrmph," I said, and coughed.

"Perhaps I may assist," suggested the thin Commissioner with a nasty look at me. "What exactly does your race do?"

"Breed bugs, I'm sure. Am head bacteriophysicist name of Lood. Am good scientist."

"And what exactly do you do with these bugs you raise?"

"Most everything."

"Your Honors," I interrupted. "At this point I propose a few simple demonstrations of what Mr. Lood and his people can do."

"May I inquire if either of my learned brethren knows any way in which we can charge Mr. Jones with rebuilding costs, if necessary?" asked the bald Commissioner.

"Your Honors, I assure you . . ."

"Proceed at your peril, Mr. Jones."

I walked over to the exhibit table and pointed to a row of jars.

"Exhibits A through G, Your Honors. Samples of food and beverages produced by my clients without raw materials and from the expert culture of bacteria."

I held up a jar full of mauve fungus. It was the most attractive example.

"I would hardly call feeding on funguses a sign of a responsible humanoid race, Mr. Jones."

"Perhaps your Honor will recall the part played by bacteria in making milk, cheese, wine, beer, bread."

The Commissioners looked at each other and nodded reluctantly. So I passed the jars up to them, secure in the knowledge they had been tested by the Alien Foods Bureau. I watched the Commissioners unscrew the lids and taste the contents somewhat hesitantly.

"Not bad," confessed the fat Commissioner eventually.

"Quite palatable."

"Of course we already have honey and similar foodstuffs, Mr. Jones."

"Naturally, Your Honor. But Mr. Lood's race can survive without extraplanetary aid. Provided they have sunshine and water, they can breed their spores and bacteria with no other resources."

"You mean," said the thin Commissioner with a dark leer, "that almost any sunny planet would do for them?"

Somewhere along the line my point seemed to have been swept away, so I added hurriedly:

"I offer this evidence purely to show the high degree of

civilization of my clients' culture, as cause why they should not be deprived of their native land."

"Oh, yus," my client agreed.

"Mr. Lood," intoned the bald Commissioner, "to stay on your present asteroid you will have to prove that your race offers something that cannot be found elsewhere in the Galactic Community. Now have these funguses of yours any special medicinal values, for example?"

"Please?"

"Can you cure diseases with them?"

"Oh, no."

"Ah," said the thin and fat Commissioners together. "Proceed, Mr. Jones."

That put Lood somewhere back behind the twentieth-century discoverers of penicillin and the myecins, and even back behind the pioneer Pasteur. Five hundred years back, in fact.

"Yes. Well. Let's see how my clients handle housing, Your Honors. I think you'll find this revolutionary. Mr. Lood?"

Lood hopped off the witness seat and trotted up to the long table normally reserved for attorneys. Lately, I have found my professional colleagues strangely reluctant to stay in court when I have a case, so Lood had the entire table to himself.

He pulled a small jar out from under the table and spread a pile of dust on the tabletop. Then he unscrewed the jar and gently poured nothing out of it onto the dust. Nothing visible, that is. But I assumed it was teeming with viruses and such.

Slowly, the dust on the table formed itself into a brick, a long eight by six by three inch brick. Lood smiled happily.

"And here, Your Honors," I said triumphantly, "here is automatic housing."

"One brick does not make a house, Mr. Jones."

"If Your Honors will just watch . . ."

The brick slowly elongated and split into two perfect bricks, lying on the table end to end.

"Mass colony action of bacteria," said Lood wisely. "Oh, yus."

The two bricks each split into two further bricks. These divided and multiplied themselves while we watched, out to the end of the table.

"I would like Your Honors to observe the way these bricks overcome natural hazards," I said, getting into my stride.

I pointed to the bricks drooping over the end of the table. A brick fell onto the floor at each end, then built itself up until it joined the line of bricks on the table, forming a perfect arch at each angle. The line on the table was now three bricks high, so I walked round and stood behind the wall.

"You see, Your Honors, suppose I need a house. I merely combine these suitable microbes and dust. And there we are, a house."

I had to stand on tiptoe to finish the sentence because of the mathematics involved. Every brick was doubling and redoubling itself in just under a minute. And the wall was getting quite impressively high.

"Mr. Jones," called one of the Commissioners.

It was not until I tried to walk round the end of the wall that I found I had been outflanked.

I ran to the nearest wall of the courtroom but the bricks got there first. I heard a rending noise that suggested the other end had gone clean through the opposite wall. As a matter of fact, I saw the astonished face of an attorney entering the main door of the Justice Building as the wall advanced towards him. Then he saw me. He grinned and waved.

I was in no mood to wave back.

"Mr. Lood, Mr. Lood," I yelled. "Can you hear me?"

"Wall too thick, yus," came a muffled answer.

And indeed it was. I had not noticed it, but the wall was expanding sideways as well. I was calculating the approximate thickness when it went up and through the roof of the courtroom.

Outside, the wall was well on the way towards completing its second simple house. This side of the wall was, that is. I could only assume it was doing something similar on the other side. There was no way of getting round and seeing, except by outstripping the wall in a sprint.

I gathered my breath and dignity and ran very rapidly down the length of the wall, round the far mounting tiers of brick, advancing now on the State Library, and back to where I had

left the Commissioners and Mr. Lood.

I was faced by a thicket of patios and arched doorways and low-roofed houses.

"Your Honors, Your Honors," I called hopefully, walking into the maze, in the general direction of what appeared to be an old and ruined war monument. It then occurred to me that this was the outer wall of the courthouse. It stood far off, pointing a stone finger to the sky, as if going down in a sea of brick for the third time.

"Your Honors, Your Honors . . ."

I met them turning a corner.

Unfortunately, they seemed to have found it necessary to crawl through a broken gap of some sort. They were very dusty and had a slightly shredded appearance.

"Ah, Mr. Jones," they said grimly, dusting each other off.

A tremendous crash announced the falling in of the roof of the State Library.

"Well," said the thin Commissioner, "he did say it was revolutionary."

I smiled politely.

"Don't giggle, Mr. Jones, or we'll hold you in contempt."

We wound out of the maze in single file. A pattering behind us announced Lood bringing up the rear.

Once we were out, and about two hundred yards ahead of the advancing walls, patios and houses, the three Commissioners turned on me.

"Mr. Jones," they said with restraint. "You will now stop this reckless building project."

I turned to Lood.

"You must stop it," I said.

"Oh, yus," he agreed, nodding happily. "Most marvelous, no. Ample housing for all and sundry. Homes for peoples. Immediate occupancy. You like the basic plan house, yus?"

"Mr. Lood," snarled the fat Commissioner. "The problem on every habitable planet so far has been to find room to build. Earth is congested . . ."

Distant crashing informed me that an unprecedented houseclearing was going on.

". . . And so are all authorized planets yet discovered. I speak for my learned brethren in saying this . . . this anthill of yours is one thing the Galactic Community can do without."

"And do without right now," added his bald colleague.

"You wish to stop?" asked Lood.

Small tears filled the periphery of his round eyes.

"Yes," I confirmed brutally. "Can you stop it?"

"Oh, yus. Must have antiseptics."

It took the fire department four hours of spraying from their copters to reduce the entire housing estate to dust. And then an even blanket of brown feathery residue lay unbroken for several acres, save here and there where the shells of previous buildings stood gauntly and accusingly.

"All bugs gone," said Lood sadly.

"But what about this mess?" demanded the bald Commissioner.

"Comes out of air. Floating particles. Process cleans air, too."

A fresh wind from across the blanket of dust came inopportunely to punctuate Mr. Lood's remark. As soon as they could talk again, the Commissioners suggested resuming in another city.

"Assuming, Mr. Jones, you wish to produce further aspects of your, hum, case."

Six red and bleary eyes stared at me from a coating of brown dust of only vaguely judicial appearance.

"I think, Your Honors, the next evidence had better be delivered in the open," I said and pointed to a nearby park.

Much, if not all, of the dust fell off us as we walked over to the small green hill in the center of the park. The birds twittered, the sun shone, the breeze was fresh; and after the Commissioners had settled on convenient tree stumps, I felt quite hopeful about the third line of evidence. Lood stood optimistically by.

"Your Honors," I said, "you are aware that Earth suffers a grave shortage of metals. Almost all economical quantities have been mined out. Yet, Your Honors—" I paused dramatically— "in the hematin of human blood alone, whose main function is to carry oxygen to the system, there is nearly twice as much iron by weight as oxygen."

"Precisely which of us, Mr. Jones, do you propose to mine first?"

I cleared my throat and let the thin Commissioner's remark pass.

"Merely making the point, Your Honor, that the metal-carrying properties of bacteria have hardly been considered."

This was stretching it a bit because selective breeding of microbes for the recovery of metals in tailings have been developed back in the 1950s. But so far as I knew, no one had carried it as far as my client race.

"Mr. Lood," I commanded.

"Just one moment, Mr. Jones," said the bald Commissioner dryly. "Let us have an outline of this *before* we start."

"Certainly, Your Honor. Mr. Lood will now extract gold from a sample of ocean water we have obtained."

I signaled to the waiting carrier and it came trundling softly over the grass and deposited a large tank on the grass.

"Genuine untouched ocean water, Your Honors," I said, slapping the tank. "Go ahead, Mr. Lood."

The little fellow hopped up to the side of the tank and emptied another invisible horde from a test tube into the water.

We waited.

"Oh, yus," he said.

And there on the bottom of the tank was an unmistakable sludge of metallic gold, shining speckled in the rays of sunlight bending through the water.

I scooped out a sample and handed it round for the Commissioners to inspect.

"Subject to analysis," grunted the fat one, "this certainly seems to be gold."

"Of course, there is no reason why this should not be done on Earth, as a starting point."

The thin Commissioner paused and looked at my client.

"Does this process affect fish?"

"Oh, yus," said Lood. "Kills all parasites. Fish, reptiles, and such."

"Thank you," said the Commissioner dryly.

Mr. Lood looked at me apologetically.

"My people too small to tolerate fish," he explained. "Fish most dangerous wild beasts. Oh, yus."

"Never mind," I reassured him. "Your Honors, I feel the court will take a more favorable view of the dry-land operation, then. Taking place as it does in the bowels of the earth, there is no danger to valuable livestock. And here we can demonstrate, for example, simple aluminum extraction, by the progressive reduction and oxidation and reduction of bacteria on a molecular scale.

"I hope," I added, "this experiment will produce visible evidence of this great boon to mankind, though I must ask Your Honors to watch closely."

Lood produced another test tube, pressed a small hole in the grass with his finger and emptied the tube. The hole darkened.

We all bent over to watch.

Nothing happened.

"Perhaps a dud batch?" I asked eventually.

"Oh, no," said Lood.

We peered intently into the small hole without seeing anything.

Then a faint wisp of steam came out of the hole. I walked over the grass, picked up a long twig, walked back and thrust it into the hole. I could not touch bottom, so something was going on down there.

The edges of the hole began to gleam with white metal. I was about to explain the alumina content of common clay, when the thin Commissioner and the tree stump he was sitting on went down with a whistling sound into a sudden pit that opened beneath him.

I only just caught the third and last Commissioner in time. We watched his tree stump sinking out of sight together.

The ground began to quiver uneasily.

"Let us get out of here with all haste."

I followed the direction of the court with proper professional zeal. And we just made it to the safe stressed-concrete surface of the old freeway when the park melted completely into a stark framework of aluminum. Seated in the middle and peering at us through the aluminum cage were the other two

Commissioners. They did not seem particularly happy.

Around them in a widening belt there opened up a pit of gleaming aluminum, melting, so to speak, towards the horizon on all sides.

"You realize, I suppose, Mr. Jones," said the bald Commissioner beside me, "that your client is in the process of eating up the Earth." He breathed heavily.

Lood was beaming and hopping up and down at the success of his experiment. I touched him in the general area of a shoulder. He looked at me.

"No," I said firmly, shaking my head.

"No?"

"No!"

His round eyes became tearful and his little green body shook.

"Oh, dear. Oh, dear. Oh, dear."

"Antiseptics?" I asked.

"Oh, yus," he confirmed sadly.

Very fortunately, the fire department was still observing my client—and me, I suspected afterwards, ridiculous as that may seem.

This time it took them several hours of deep spraying and drilling to confine the area. A vast saucer of aluminum remained.

"Useful for signaling to stars, oh, yus?" asked Lood, hopefully.

"Oh, no," I said.

A threatening cough made me turn round to see the three Commissioners staring at me.

"Mr. Jones . . ."

" . . . you have now destroyed the Courthouse, the Public Library and five city blocks . . ."

". . . and buried them under a filthy layer of dust . . ."

". . . and reduced a park into a great garbage pit . . ."

". . . we therefore refuse your claim and give you and your client six hours to get off Earth . . ."

". . . and kindly do not trouble to advise us where the Space Council moves you. We will sleep more soundly for believing that it will be many, many light-years away."

And they turned and walked away, leaving me with my client—and, apparently, my traveling companion.

A quiet and suppressed sobbing made me turn and look at Lood. He wept dolefully.

"We have nothing," he said. "Oh, no. We have nothing to offer. Nothing that you humans want."

"Well," I said, "that's the way it goes sometimes."

And what, I wondered, was I going to do for a living now?

"Free food," gulped Lood. "Free housing. Free gold and metals. We had all hoped so much from this. Oh, yus."

There did not seem any point in telling him his people were several hundred years too late. Once upon a time he would have been hailed as a savior of a starving and poor human race, a great benefactor of mankind. Now he was just a nuisance. And I was another for letting him loose.

"Well," I assured him, "you have got one guest until they shift you off your asteroid. Me. Free food and housing will suit me fine. And maybe we'll find some very backward part of the Galaxy where they need gold and such.

"It's a pity," I added, as we started to walk towards the spaceport, "that you can't control these bacteria of yours."

"Can control."

"It didn't look like it, my friend."

"Oh, yus. Can control bodily leucocytes, corpuscles and such. Perfect cell replacement easy."

I looked down at him.

"If it's all that easy," I said, "I suppose your old men can run faster than your houses."

"No old men," said Lood.

"Well, old whatever-you-are's."

"No old. Not die. Oh, yus. Perfect cell replacement."

I stood very still.

"Do you mean you never die?" I asked.

"Oh, yus. Never die."

"Can teach?" I asked.

"Oh, yus. Most simple," smiled Lood. "Can teach all men not die. Not ever."

But I was off running after the three Commissioners, yelling until they stopped and stood waiting for me. . . .